HAND OVER HAND

written by Alma Fullerton

illustrated by Renné Benoit

Second Story Press

On the shores
of a Filipino fishing village
an old banca boat rocks
as waves lick its keel.

WHOOSH,
    WHOOSH,
        WHOOSH.

Nina watches it from her chair
by the drying rack.
Maybe today, she will convince
Lolo to take her with him.

As they load the boat
for a day of fishing,
Nina asks, "Can I go with you?"

"Fishing makes for a long, hard day,"
Lolo answers.

"A boat is not the place for a girl.
Your job is on shore."

"But I have no more fish to dry,
and with two of us we can catch
twice as many fish to sell
at the market tomorrow," Nina says.

"You'll bait your own hook?" Lolo asks.

"Yes!" Nina answers.

"And remove your own fish?" Lolo asks.

"Yes! Yes!" Nina answers.

"Okay, we will try it. Just for today."

As the sun rises,
they push the old banca boat out
past the night fishermen coming in.

The fishermen scoff and call,
"You old fool. Girls can't fish.
Their place is on shore."

"We shall see," Lolo says.

The old banca boat
glides across the bay.

Lolo in front,
Nina behind,
their paddles
dipping gracefully
into the dark water

PLICK,
   PLICK,
      PLICK.

When they reach the fishing grounds
Lolo shows Nina how to bait the hooks
and drop the lines.

He shows her how to jig
to attract the fish
and how to set the hook
when there's a tug on the line.

Lolo's movements flow
fast and smooth,

hand
    over
        hand,

as he brings up the line
with a fish on the end.

But there are no
tugs on Nina's line.

As the sun climbs,
sending ripples of golden light
along the sea,
Lolo's buckets begin to fill.

Hand
    over
        hand.

Fish
after
fish.

But still there are no
tugs on Nina's line.

"I must be doing something wrong.
Maybe those fishermen were right.
Girls can't fish," Nina says.

"Posh! The fish can't tell you're a girl."

As the sun sits high in the sky,
Lolo's buckets are half full.

Hand
over
hand,

fish
after
fish.

But there are no
tugs on Nina's line.

"Maybe my bait is gone," she says.

Nina brings her line in, just like Lolo did.

Hand
    over
        hand,

letting it pile between her feet
on the floor of the boat.

Until the line

ZIPS

through her fingers
and unravels from the floor.

Lolo jumps
and wraps the end of the line
around the bench so it doesn't
head out to sea.

The line tugs,
jerking the boat.

"Brace yourself," Lolo says,
"and bring it back."

Hand
     over
          hand.

ZING!

"It's too big!
Can you do it?" Nina asks.
"I might lose it."

"This is your fight," Lolo says.
"You can do it, Nina."

As the sun rests
just above the mountains
in a red and orange sky,
Nina fights with the fish.

Hand
    over
        hand.
ZIP
    after
        ZING…

…until she guides the fish
close enough to haul it in.

"Nina you're a fisher-*person*
through and through!"
Lolo lights the lanterns,
and the old banca boat
glides toward home.

"You're out late, old man,"
a night fisherman calls.

"Nina had a fighter," Lolo answers.

"We warned you that girls can't fish."
Lolo smiles as the fishermen
look into his old banca boat.

"How'd a little girl bring *that* in?"
one of the men asks.

"Hand
over
hand,"

Nina tells them.

For my Dad.
—A.F.

For Emmett and Amelia.
—R.B.

―――――――――――

Library and Archives Canada Cataloguing in Publication

Fullerton, Alma, author
Hand over hand / by Alma Fullerton ;
illustrated by Renné Benoit.

ISBN 978-1-77260-015-5 (hardback)

I. Benoit, Renné, illustrator II. Title.

PS8611.U45H35 2017   jC813'.6   C2016-906762-9

Printed and bound in China

Second Story Press gratefully acknowledges the support of the Ontario Arts Council and the Canada Council for the Arts for our publishing program. We acknowledge the financial support of the Government of Canada through the Canada Book Fund.

ONTARIO ARTS COUNCIL
CONSEIL DES ARTS DE L'ONTARIO
an Ontario government agency
un organisme du gouvernement de l'Ontario

Canada Council   Conseil des Arts
for the Arts   du Canada

Funded by the Government of Canada
Financé par le gouvernement du Canada | Canadä

Published by
Second Story Press
20 Maud Street, Suite 401
Toronto, Ontario, Canada
M5V 2M5
www.secondstorypress.ca